Publisher's Note: This is a work of fiction. Names, characters, places, and incidents are a product of the author's imagination. Locales and public names are sometimes used for atmospheric purposes. Any resemblance to actual people, living or dead, or to businesses, companies, events, institutions, or locales is coincidental.

Edited by Aquila Editing

Cover Designer: Cover Girl Design

## Hello from Abby!

Thanks for picking up my book! If you want to check out more of my titles and get some free stuff, please visit my author page at www.authorabbyknox.com.

Happy reading!

# CAKE Walk

## ABBY KNOX

## Summary

Cara

I found the perfect spot to sell my cakes for my preschool's fundraiser: smack in the middle of the town's most exclusive gated community. That has everything to do with where the money is, and probably nothing to do with catching a glimpse of my dad's gorgeous best friend, Michael.

Michael

I don't remember how I ended up as the enforcer for the homeowners association, but I truly give no crap if some cute blonde wants to sell cakes on my street to raise money for the local preschool. When I discover that the cute blonde is my best friend's daughter, I have to enforce the rules to make Cara go away. Far, far away, before I act on my feelings. Because my feelings are wrong…right?

# Chapter One

Michael

THE POUNDING on my front door matches the pounding in my head. I roll to the empty side of my California king and shove the cool, unused pillow over my ears and eyes to blot out the rude interruption to my whiskey-soaked slumber.

The knocking continues, now with fresh urgency.

Emitting a groan mixed with a yawn, I rub my blood-shot eyes. In my season of life, a man my age should be too busy morning-fucking his wife even to notice some idiot knocking at 7:52 a.m. on a Saturday. A pair of soft thighs covering my ears seems like a most effective and pleasur-able way to block out noise.

No such luck for me; the knocking continues.

I could ignore it. I shouldn't; it could be HOA business, and I hate HOA business. On the other hand, maybe it's not that. Perhaps I'll get lucky. I grin ruefully, fantasizing that it could be the woman of my dreams knocking on my door. Wouldn't that be the bee's knees to fall in love at first sight at the age of 46?

Harrumphing, I sit up and look at the front door camera that's connected to my phone. It's my neighbor, Mrs. Hurley. Local busybody—not the woman of my dreams.

I shuffle to the front door and open it four inches precisely, not enough for her to stick her foot inside and "take just a quick moment" of my time to complain about the height of someone's lawn or the peeling paint on someone's mailbox.

"Yeah," I grunt.

If she's annoyed by my abruptness and appearance—I didn't bother checking a mirror before answering the door in only my pajama bottoms—her oversized sunglasses and Botox camouflage that fact.

"Mr. Brennan. I'm sorry to wake you—"

"Are you?" I ask though she doesn't hear it or acknowledge my question because she keeps right on yapping.

"—but everyone is asking, did you issue a permit for this…this yard sale today? Because I don't recall voting on a special exemption."

I rub the pads of my thumb and forefinger into my eyelids to clear the cobwebs caused by too much whiskey the night before and because I have no idea what Mrs. Hurley is babbling about.

I also don't like the way she said "yard sale" as if the idea of it is beneath her, like it's equal to a tick on the tush of her obnoxious little terrier.

"Huh?" is all I can muster in the way of requesting more information.

Impatiently, Mrs. Hurley rams my door open wide; the force of it catches me off guard, and I stumble backward.

Those new barre classes at the clubhouse are working for Mrs. Hurley's core strength.

Bleary-eyed, I look past her and follow her pointing beige talons.

"Huh," I remark, staring at the unusual sight at my best friend Bill's driveway.

"Is that all you have to say, Mr. President?"

How I ever got roped into serving as the HOA president, I'll never know. The velvet fog of retirement made me agree to "volunteer" for one thing or another, and as a newbie to Fox Chase life, the affluent suburbanites got their claws into me early. But I intend to weasel out as soon as possible.

"No. I'd also say that's not something you see every day in Fox Chase." A line of people stretches from Bill's curb at the corner of Vixen Court and around Hunter Drive. Cars are easing their way around each other, drivers looking for places to park where there are none.

"There is a Hyundai parked in front of my house right now. A Hyundai!" Mrs. Hurley is chapping my last nerve. Not to mention her colossal beach bag is partially blocking my view of something particularly pleasing.

In Bill's driveway, a soft, curvy female wearing a yellow sundress scurries around, arranging colorful items on long tables. The set-up does sort of look like a yard sale, but not exactly. It seems a little more festive than the yard sales my dad used to let me tag along to, while he scoped out deals on rusty hammers and socket wrenches. This ain't that. I see balloons and cutesy little pendant banners in bright colors. Gingham tablecloths. There's one of those portable awnings set up at a checkout station, presumably to keep the sun at bay from all that skin she's showing in that sundress. It's all very quaint. But none of the charm comes close to that damn dress that taunts the hell out of me at the moment; its spaghetti straps show off her long, tanned arms and delicate collarbones; the length of the yellow chiffon hangs just short enough to reveal a pair of solid and feminine thighs. Mrs. Hurley is still pointing, so I feel free to keep staring, noticing the way this strange woman's butt jiggles under the wispy fabric. She looks as delicious as lemon meringue, and the thought of lemons—and her lemons in my mouth—makes my mouth water.

It's been way too long since I grabbed on to a soft, squeezable bottom. I bet those thighs of hers would do a more-than-adequate job of noise canceling. Better still, those thighs look strong enough to snap my neck efficiently. I silently groan at the thought of dying with a smile on my glazed-over face.

Mrs. Hurley insists on interrupting my little death fantasy. "Mr. Brennan!"

"I'm going; I'm going. Keep your Lululemons on," I bark.

I shuffle past Mrs. Hurley and meander down my front steps and across my lawn, my eyes examining the wavy blonde bob on Sundress Lady. That's not Bill's wife, Corrina. I'd be a world-class jerk if I found myself popping a boner over my best friend's wife. But this woman's hair is similar. A visiting sister-in-law from out of town? Who is she? She doesn't live there, as far as I know—I kind of wish she did.

"Mr. Brennan?!"

Mrs. Hurley is still on my property, demanding attention yet again. Grunting, "Yeah?" I turn around to see her now pointing at my bare chest. "Aren't you going to get dressed first?"

"Avert your eyes if you must, Mrs. Hurley. But keep

pointing at my chest like that, I'm going to have to register a complaint with the Fox Chase HOA sexual harassment department."

She splutters and trails off, "There's no…such department…I didn't mean to…."

I turn and continue on my way over to Bill's house, my eyes locked on the pretty blonde with the cute and very busy ass, still arranging and decorating and looking stressed. Maybe I can be of help with that. With selling… whatever that is. Girl Scout cookies? Shit, yes, I'll buy every last box and effectively put an end to this whole shindig. Everyone wins. Mrs. Hurley gets to shuffle off to the club-house pool with a slightly less sour look on her face, pretty Sundress Lady gets some quick cash, and maybe I get a phone number.

The aroma hits me first, and I understand what's going on here. This isn't a yard sale but a bake sale. The first scent that strikes me is cherry pie, and I immediately begin to salivate. Maybe I'll get something sweet for breakfast from her to counteract this hangover.

The next thing that hits my senses is her voice. But it doesn't make me drool; it hits me with a dose of reality right across the face. "Now, now, everyone. I'm not quite ready yet. The sale starts at 8 a.m. And it's only 7:55. I've still got a batch of brownies in the oven."

Her words stop me dead in my tracks and turn my throat to the Sahara Desert. I know this person. She's Cara Williams, the soft-spoken second daughter of Bill and Corrina.

If I thought I would be an asshole for popping a boner for my best friend's wife, this is an entirely more profound level of asshole. Bill's daughter. The sweetest, most intro-verted of all five of the Williams girls, at that. As I recall, the one I used to see on my early morning runs in the city. I would spot her reading her books under a tree in the park near my condo before school.

I should turn around and go back inside, take a cold shower, drink some water, eat some protein to soak up the remnants of this alcohol. I used to eat at a fantastic little restaurant near my condo for post-hangover chilaquiles. There's nothing like that around here, and I don't know how to cook. I could order some Taco Bell to be delivered. Not the same—not even close—but maybe the aroma of a crunch-wrap will be enough to drive Mrs. Hurley off my porch.

I could do that. But then that would leave poor Cara under the scrutiny of Mrs. Hurley and any number of other neighborhood busybodies who might complain about the Williamses to the HOA. I don't want that to happen, either.

I have to do the right thing. I always do the right thing by the family that has taken me in on Thanksgivings and Christmases.

As I approach, I can't help but notice Cara looks very different from the painfully shy high school valedictorian to whom I'd cut a sizable check four years ago. The angelic girl is selling cakes on her parents' front lawn.

This simply won't do. It won't do for me to be having thoughts about her rump, and her thighs, and her cleavage in that dress, even if the message hasn't reached my wide-awake cock yet this morning. And it won't do for her to be going to any effort to collect money for anything. It doesn't sit right with me. Not across the street from my house. And not when I, her Uncle Michael, can easily cut a check or whatever it is that she might need.

Uncle Michael. God. I'm a sick, desperate man.

I'm going to put a stop to this. Now. I've got to make

her go away. Out of sight, out of mind, right? Besides, I don't like the way people are so eager to hand her money. There must be fifty people lined up and more coming.

I'm putting a stop to this circus once and for all.

Why? Because I'm the motherfucking HOA president, and I have to enforce the rules.

# Chapter Two

Cara

A HUNDRED GOURMET chocolate chip cookies, seventeen Granny Smith apple hand-pies with Saigon cinnamon, and nineteen cakes of varying flavors with colorful handmade icing flowers are attractively spread out over all the banquet tables I could find in my parents' storage locker. The other pre-K teachers helped me make fun signage, festive balloon centerpieces, and eye-catching banners. My sister Cherise contributed a few batches of cupcakes in between her busy days at culinary school. My parents helped by letting me use their yard—smack in the middle of the wealthiest neighborhood in this suburb. But if I'm honest, the most significant help of all was name-dropping my brother-in-law.

Famous British chef Phillip Wildwood married my older sister Chloe last year, as luck would have it. I may have implied on the Facebook event that Phillip himself had donated cakes to this fundraiser. While that might not be one hundred percent true, the cakes I made came straight from Phillip's many cookbooks. He'd permitted me to use his image on the promotional materials, which, let's face it, is pretty eye-catching for anyone in the market for baked goods.

So it's a good thing I know how to bake. And it's a good thing I know how to use all the top-tier ingredients that Phillip was kind enough to donate; he couldn't bear the thought of anyone selling cakes based on his recipes using basic supermarket ingredients. Bless his snooty British heart.

Mom was livid when Chloe announced she was not coming home after meeting Phillip in England. Dad was taken aback but mostly okay with it, realizing he had no leg to stand on if he opposed the match, having built up Chloe's confidence with the entire scheme. "I didn't think it would work," was one memorable line from the toast Dad gave at the state-side marriage reception. Now, anyone who looked askance at the age difference has come around because everyone can see how much he loves and takes care of Chloe. Her pregnancy, and Phillip's willingness to fly family members back and forth to England anytime she needs them, has also softened everyone toward him, even if he is at times a bit prickly and difficult to read, except to Chloe, and to our mother. It might not be the most traditional mother-son-in-law relationship, with my mother being a year younger than Phillip, but he dotes on her almost as much as he does Chloe.

Diana, my younger sister by a year, is here to help with the sale as part of her court-ordered community service, but she's helped chiefly by eating the merchandise. I snatch a scone out of her hand. "What are you doing?" I hiss.

"I'm hungry!" she defends through a mouthful of lemon poppyseed.

"Then go inside and raid Mom's fridge like you always do."

"Hurtful," she says, with a playful smile on her lips.

I roll my eyes. "Every bite you sneak is a dollar taken away from my kids. Kids you are supposed to be helping as part of your community service, remember?"

"Your kids, huh? I don't see any kids anywhere for me to help."

I cross my arms. "As soon as you stop damaging property, maybe grow up, become a judge, then you can decide what sort of community service is best for career criminals such as yourself."

"Career criminals don't get sentenced to volunteer at snooty schools in the suburbs."

"Would you rather be picking up trash on the side of the highway? Because this is a pretty sweet gig. Any anyway, special-needs four-year-olds deserve playground time too."

Diana squints at me like I'm dim. "Of course they do. But why are we doing this here, at Mom and Dad's house?"

I sigh and explain it to her again. "Because Mom and Dad have a big yard. And this neighborhood is where the money is."

Diana arcs a brow at me and says, "Uh-huh," as if she's reading me silently.

"And because Mom has a huge kitchen. So it's more convenient."

"Right," she says thoughtfully.

"And it's where I live. Because I can't afford a place on my own on a teacher assistant salary."

"Yeah."

"And it's close to Cherise's culinary school, and she and her classmates donated the cupcakes."

"And?"

"And what?!"

"And it wouldn't have anything to do with the proximity to the big wiener across the street."

I could blame my instant beet-red face on this brisk fall morning, but there's no point. Diana sees everything. And she loves to be in the know. Typical middle child.

"God, you're tactless! That's not it at all!" I splutter.

Diana gasps at my indignation. "You are so obvious! You've been obsessed since you were thirteen!" she stage-whispers.

I set down the final pies fresh from the oven on the gingham tablecloth. "This whole crass subject could have been avoided if you hadn't read my diary when we were kids."

Diana chuckles through a mouthful of peanut butter fudge. "This could have been even better avoided if I hadn't set my ex's car on fire. But to be fair, your crush on our Uncle Mike traumatized me into this life of crime."

"I hate you," I chirp in a sing-song way that only sisters can say without hurting each other.

"People always hate the truth-tellers," Diana says.

I roll my eyes. Diana might be the most Aries who ever Aries-ed. "If I give you some peanut butter fudge and sign your form for the judge, will you take it inside, stick it in your face hole and never say the words 'Uncle Mike' to me ever again?"

Diana considers this. "Done." She grabs the plate of fudge she's been nibbling at for the last hour and goes inside. I love my sister, but she's a handful. She's always been the wildest, snarkiest, and at the center of most Williams family drama. You'd think that middle child would have gotten herself enough attention by now, but that well is bottomless.

Once she's gone, I look around me and wonder if Diana was right. Maybe I did set this whole thing up just to be closer to Michael. To maybe get a glimpse of him. Just like the way I did when I was in high school. In my senior year, I started going to city college twice a week. The downtown campus was just up the road from his condo, and I might have staked out where he would go running in the morning. I was so embarrassed when he'd spotted me.

And when he handed me that huge check at my high school graduation party, I chickened out. I was eighteen, had pined for him for five years. I looked at the amount and realized just how powerful this man was, just how out of my league. Sure, we live in a fancy gated neighborhood, but we're far from wealthy. My parents needed a big house for us five girls and jumped on a bank-owned Fox Chase house during the mortgage crisis. They got the house for a song and have worked hard to fix it up. We and others like us who bought the houses here for cheap have never quite fit into this neighborhood. This is why Daddy convinced Michael to move here, so he'd have someone to golf with now that he was nearing retirement from his house-flipping business.

*Ugh. Why am I torturing myself?*

Diana has been having fun with one boyfriend after another for years. I'll bet she lost her virginity at 15, with as much as she sneaked out of the house. I don't see anything wrong with that. Maybe she had the right idea.

Maybe I'm pathetic, carrying a torch for someone almost as old as our father. Perhaps I'm sick.

Is that why I dressed like this?

I check the time on my phone, 7:59 a.m. My motive doesn't matter now: time to sell some cakes. "All right, folks. I'm ready for you. Come and get it!"

Behind me, a deep, male voice sears the skin on the

back of my neck and makes the backs of my knees gush with sweat.

"How much for the cherry?"

Wide-eyed, I whirl around and come face to chest with Michael Brennan. Face to bare chest. Oh no. Oh my. This isn't happening.

There he is, my dad's best friend, bare of chest, wearing blue plaid flannel pajama bottoms, and looking mussed and sleepy and sexy as hell.

"Hi, Cara."

I'm not prepared for him, nor am I prepared for the way he says my name. Like The Witcher just woke up with a croaky morning voice and wants me to join him in the bath. Uh, yes, please. All you need to do is ask. A wrinkle from the bedsheets still marks him across his shoulder, slashing down across his sternum. Wild images invade my stupid horny skull, involving Michael asleep, tangled up naked in sheets.

"Hi. Hi…"

"Michael."

"I know," I laugh, slapping myself on the forehead. "Of course I know you."

My cheeks heat at the intensity of the way he's looking at me while his Adam's apple bobs.

"I haven't seen you since your high school graduation party."

I nod dumbly. *Don't comment on his shirtlessness. Don't do it.* "You had on more clothes then, as I recall," I say, actually dipping my forehead to gesture at one small erect man nipple. It's surrounded by soft salt and pepper fuzz that I would love to cuddle up to. Or grab tight to while I climb the man like a tree and grind on him.

Oh god, what is he doing to me? If he only knew the

thoughts I was having about that chest, those lips, that slight scruff of beard.

This man has no idea—none—how much he's appeared in my fantasies over the years. So much so that I've never entertained the thought of anyone else. It's preposterous, holding out for a man twice my age. But then, Chloe gives me hope. No fantasy is too ridiculous for the Williams girls. Some might say we like our men unattainable. I would say we have big dreams.

One of those big dreams is threatening to push its way out the fly of his pajama pants.

*Don't look at the tent. Don't look at it. Don't you dare.*

"Nice tent," he says.

"What?" I say, horrified, and my eyes do the thing they're not supposed to do. They look down. My eyes can't look away from the morning wood.

His slightly bloodshot eyes are still as gorgeous as ever with those delicate crow's feet that smile down at me. Michael gestures toward the cashier station next to me. He meant the awning tent. Not the…other kind.

"Oh," I say, laughing. "Yeah. I went a little bit overboard, but it's all for the kids."

"How much for the cherry pie?"

"Five dollars each."

He looks incredulous. "That's it?"

I give an exaggerated wave of my arm like the woman on *The Price is Right.* "Well, they're small and portable. You can take them right back to your house. Where the clothes are, I presume."

He blinks at me.

I stammer, "A-and we have a fine selection of layer cakes as well."

"I guess I'm pretty hungry. I'll try some cake," he says.

He's looking at me so strangely, like he wants to say something, but he's holding back.

I stammer. "I can't cut you a slice of cake unless you buy the entire cake."

"Fine. I'll take all of them."

"Mr. Brennan?" I look up at him, blocking the sun from my eyes. Politely, he steps sideways to block the glare for me.

"How old are you, Cara?"

"Twenty-three."

"I think you can call me Michael now," he says.

I shake my head at my silly self. "Of course. Force of habit." What I don't say is that force of habit has nothing to do with my good manners and everything to do with shouting "Mr. Brennan!" every time I come when using my vibrator. And not just shout his name. I named my vibrator Mr. Brennan. *I know. I know!*

"Now, Michael, what is it that I can get for you?"

"All of them. Everything. How much for the entire inventory?"

I bluster, "What? Why?"

Ever the businessman, he peers down at me. "You drive a hard bargain. I'll pay twice the asking price."

I shift my weight nervously. "This…this isn't an auction, Mr. Brennan…Michael. I don't think you understand…."

He sighs. "Fine. Triple. For every cake you got."

I can't believe he's doing this. "That's not your wallet in those pajama pockets, is it?"

*Don't look down, Cara. You've seen that bulge before that time your family went out on Michael's boat.*

"Fine. But I have dibs. I'll be right back."

He leaves, and I expect Michael to come back fully dressed. I exhale in relief that I don't have to face all that bare skin again, or all that lovely fuzz, or his dick's outline. I mean, really. How dare he?

A sweet older woman approaches the checkout station with a fistful of tens. "I'll take the carrot cake, dear."

I stutter, "Ah, well…you see…."

She furrows her brow. "What's the problem, honey? Just the cake, that's all."

I glance over at the nine-inch round layer cake decorated with chopped walnuts on the sides and orange carrot shapes frosted in a circle like a crown around the top.

Looking over at Michael's house, I begin to doubt he's coming back. He's probably toying with me. Maybe he's known all along about my childish crush, and he's messing around now. Taunting me with his money, reminding me how out of my league he is.

"Of course," I say to the grandmotherly woman, taking her cash and placing it in the cash box. I set about boxing up her cake, and then I text Diana to come outside and help carry the cake to the woman's car.

"Thank you, dear. This cake looks lovely," she says. "You've done a tremendous amount of work."

I shrug and smile. "It's all about the kids."

Diana comes outside at the exact moment I see Michael's door opening. I hurriedly give her instructions and tell her to follow the woman to her car.

Diana does as she's told—thank god—but gives me the stink eye. "Alright, I'm going. Calm your panties."

I roll my eyes. "So gross."

She wags her head and follows the woman down the street, just as Michael reappears. Still shirtless. Still in those godforsaken flannel plaid pajama pants.

Diana swivels her head around from Michael's direction back to me and mouths, "Oh my god!"

I purse my lips and wave my arms wildly for her to

keep moving. And hopefully, disappear forever into the ether. Maybe then I'll have some peace.

Michael's not just got a wallet in hand, but his open checkbook.

"I see you couldn't wait for me." He winks, readying his pen. "Coulda got triple the asking price. Now, how much for everything here?"

I shake my head in amazement. He's not messing around. I think he's unaware of the effect his half-naked body has on me. I swallow, my throat still dry as a bone.

"If I sold all of this? Probably around eight hundred dollars. Including all the cookies and cupcakes, too."

He drops his pen and stares down at me. "What did you say this was for?"

"I didn't," I say. "But it's for a new pre-K playground. Special needs pre-K, to be exact."

"So you need a lot more than eight hundred."

I stammer. "W-well, yes. I have three more things planned for this year, and hopefully, we'll—"

He shakes his head. "Nope. Here."

He scribbles out an amount and tears off the check. When he hands it to me, I goggle at the amount. It's five figures.

"This is too much."

"On the contrary. Have your sisters, or whoever is around, deliver everything to my house. I'll be having a shower."

I find my boldness, and I ask, "Why are you doing this?"

As he walks away, he shouts over his shoulder, "Because I can't let people give you money in the street. It's HOA rules, not mine. I'm just protecting you from trouble. Everyone here can go home!" he shouts.

People are grumbling and starting to ask questions,

pressing me to let them pay for their cakes and cookies they've been browsing.

I turn back to the crowd and tell them, "I'm so sorry folks. Mr. Brennan over there just bought me out. Thank you for coming, and I'm sorry."

By the sound of protest, you'd think I'd just told them all they were banned from buying cake ever again, for life.

Michael has created more trouble for me by showing off with his money.

And he's gonna get it.

# Chapter Three

Michael

I'VE BITTEN off more than I can chew.

All the cake zombies who were lined up down the street are now lined up down my front walk.

What the hell did I do?

Cara sees me peeking through the blinds, and she's standing there with one hand on her jutted-out hip, looking slightly sassy and amused.

I've known this girl since she was a baby--when Bill, Corrina, and I started college together. Bill's second-oldest daughter hasn't lived with Bill and Corrina since she went off to college herself...traveling or working or studying... and now, apparently, she's back.

The universe is playing some sick joke on me as punishment for not putting myself out there in the dating world. I was engaged once upon a time, and after that disaster, I've only had more disasters because of...some particular needs.

And now, my self-imposed drought is causing me to look at someone I know in a very different light, and that's not fair to her.

It's my fault for not keeping closer tabs on these girls. If I'd socialized more, paid more attention to my friends, I wouldn't be lusting after a woman half my age.

Against all my judgment, I open the door. They might as well have pitchforks and torches, the way they're looking at me. "How can I help you folks?"

"We wanted to buy those cakes."

Diana pushes past them with a rolling cart full of boxed cakes.

The man at the front of the line says, "We heard Phillip Wildwood himself donated these cakes." The name rings a bell, and then I realize that's the famous British baker who married Bill's oldest daughter last year. I recall having my assistant pick out a gift from the registry and ship it. The thank you card with the wedding photo is on my fridge. Perfect exchange of pleasantries for me. I didn't have to attend a wedding, and they got a set of high thread-count sheets.

"How much do you want for it?" I ask as Diana wheels the cakes into my kitchen and begins unloading. Cara follows behind her with another cart packed full of cake boxes.

"What?"

"How much will you pay for one of those cakes?" I ask the man at the head of the crowd.

"What are you going to do, price gouge us?" he asks.

"No, but you came here to buy cakes. Anything you want to pay me to get a cake, I'll donate back to the school."

And that's how I spent the rest of my Saturday morning: selling cakes out of my damn house in my pajama pants.

This is a punishment from the universe for lusting after my best friend's 24-year-old daughter.

# Chapter Four

Cara

At first, it's amusing, what he's doing.

And then he hands me the second check of the morning.

The crowd has gone, Diana had helped me deliver all the cakes and has hightailed it back to the house. It seems he has sold every last cake back to the shoppers. I'm standing in Michael's doorway, half in and half out.

"This is insane. You already paid for everything and more," I say, shaking the check at him.

He pours himself a cup of coffee and offers me one. I shake my head.

"Yeah, but it didn't quite go as planned. The only way I could make those people go away was to let them buy the damn cakes. I couldn't very well profit off my little scheme, now, could I?"

The light in his eye lights a fire below my waist. I lick my lips.

I check the amount on the check. "Wait a minute; this is thirty dollars less than the first check. Not that I'm complaining, but…."

"I kept one for myself."

Curious, I ask, "Which one?"

"It reminded me of you."

I look, and on the kitchen table is the lemon blueberry layer cake. "The one with the yellow sugar daisies all over it."

Smiling at him, I open my mouth to speak, but the words don't come.

"I think we're done here. Tell Bill and Corrina to come on over for cake later when they get home."

I bite my lip. "Mom and Dad are in Barbados for their 25th anniversary. Hence why they especially didn't mind me using their yard for the sale."

He eyes me. "Barbados, huh?" He looks a little strange, a little sad. "Imagine being 46 and celebrating 25 years of marriage."

I nod. "They're my parents, so, yes, I can imagine."

We share an awkward silence, and I'm not sure where to look. His stomach growls, and I have an urge to putter around his kitchen and fix him an omelet. Finally, he says, "So I'm sure you've got things to do. School papers to grade and such."

I laugh. "We don't grade papers in pre-K."

"Oh. Well, I'm sure you have things to do. Like, put tables away."

"Diana can do it," I say with a smirk. "Community service."

"Do I wanna know?"

I laugh and shake my head.

"She might need you to supervise."

"Mr. B, Michael, I'm not her parole officer. She's a big girl. Like me."

Michael's jaw ticks. "Well…it was good seeing you again, Cara."

He seems as if he's trying to get me to walk out this door. If he's so worried about being alone with me, he should put on a shirt.

"Let me thank you properly." I take a step toward him. His eyes go wide, and he backs away from me.

"You have to go. You don't need to thank me."

"Why don't you let me cook some breakfast for you."

He dabs the corner of his eye, strangely.

"Because it would be wrong."

"Wrong?"

"Wrong, unseemly. For me to have you in my house by yourself." He backs up again, now gripping the edge of the countertop. His knuckles are as white as the marble.

"Nonsense, I've been alone with you lots of times."

"Not since you grew up into—" He blinks, darting his eyes around the room aimlessly.

"Into what?" What in the world could he mean? Surely he doesn't mean… That would be too good to be true. I've dreamt about it, hoped for it. Sure, I'm here offering to cook breakfast, begging, pleading inside just to be close to him. But I never thought that he would reciprocate my feelings.

Finally, he pushes off the countertop and points at me. The look on his face is so severe, I flinch. "Into twelve different kinds of mind-blowing sex in a sundress."

I gasp and blurt before I can correct myself. "Mr. Brennan."

He takes a step toward me, and slowly I begin backing toward the door. My mind tells me to turn and run, but my body says *stay*.

"I'm sorry," he says softly, holding up his palms in apology. "I didn't mean to scare you."

I shake my head and whisper, "I'm not scared. I think we need to unpack what you just said."

He closes in another step, and now my back faces the street, the door still open, thanks to Diana wheeling the carts away without stopping to close the door.

"I shouldn't have said that." He towers over me in the open doorway, his shoulders level with my nose. I can smell his masculine scent. Move one inch, and I'd be burying my face in that expanse of silky chest hair. I swallow hard. It's time to tell him the truth.

"I think you needed to say that," I say. "Just like I need to say some things."

My eyes drift upward to meet his big, soulful green eyes, his fierce expression that communicates both fear and something like desperation.

"Michael, it's not just about the money. I like you. I've always liked you."

A curse escapes him. "That's sweet of you to say. Really. But when I look at you, I think about fucked up shit."

I know he doesn't mean to hurt me, but that stings. "Don't call it that. Please. It's not fucked up. I'm a grown woman."

"Your dad will murder me."

"No, he won't!"

Michael brings one balled fist to his mouth and presses it to his lips.

"I'm a man with powerful, grown-up needs. Physical needs. You're a perfect little, I don't know, dandelion with feelings and deep thoughts, and I don't want to sully that with...."

"What makes you think there's anything wrong with you—"

Some strange awareness stops me from saying another word. Something out of the corner of my eye, or a sixth sense that someone is watching. Or wanting attention. My eyes drift downward, and I see what it is that's making the hairs on the back of my neck stand up.

The presence is deep pink, veiny, and protruding from the fly in Michael's pajama pants.

I gasp again, this time in shock that this man's rod is poking out, winning in the fight against the loose confines of the flannel drawers.

And damn me if I don't salivate as intensely as the dampening of my untouched sex.

I swallow. "Is that…?"

He looks down. "Oh fuck!" Michael turns away from the door.

"Were you not wearing…why are you not wearing underwear?"

"I was naked before Mrs. Hurley showed up," he explains, which explains nothing. I find myself wanting to elbow Mrs. Hurley in the ribs the next time she shows up on Michael's doorstep.

"You could have thrown on undies before engaging with the public outdoors, you know."

"Look. I'm hungover; I'm not thinking straight. And to be honest, before the cake hordes started knocking down my door, I was getting ready to…never mind."

"Tell me."

"Forget it."

"Getting ready to what?"

"Cara."

"Mr. Brennan, Michael, were you about to pleasure yourself? Alone? In your bed? That's something we have in common. Well, not so much anymore since I moved back home. So little privacy. It's been…a very long time."

I know what I'm doing. I know it's especially crass for me, someone who criticizes the way her sister talks. But this feels different. I know he's looking at me differently, and he needs to know I'm grown now.

"Fuck me." His shoulder rolls as he tucks himself back into his drawers then rests one hand high against the wall. His head hangs like he's deep in a troubling thought, like he's fighting invisible demons.

"Please tell me the truth. Everyone shields me from everything shocking because they believe I'm so delicate. The truth is I'm deadly curious. I have so many questions. And I wouldn't want answers from anyone—anyone—but you, Michael."

He responds through gritted teeth. "You don't know what you're saying."

"I trust you. I know you better than you think I do. Do you remember when you used to live downtown, and you'd see me reading in the park before school?"

His voice is raspy; he raises his head to look back at me over his shoulder. "Yes."

I am fighting so hard to keep tears at bay now. If he knew the depths of my feelings. If he knew the things I could declare right now. "I went there on purpose, hoping to see you. I planned it out. I just wanted to be near you. I know, it's crazy and pathetic and—"

"Cara. Don't talk about yourself like that."

Michael turns around to face me.

"It's true. I've had a terrible crush on you my whole life. Ever since I was thirteen, I knew I wanted you to be my first kiss."

Michael chuckles. "A lot can happen in ten years. Thank god, right?"

I hold out my hand. With a confused look on his face, he hesitantly places his hand in my palm. I take it, my body sighing at the connection to his warmth, to his rough, grown-man hands. I turn it over and trace my finger around his palm. "This was the last thing I saw of you before I went to college. You gave me a check, but I didn't care about that. You shook my hand and held it briefly in both of yours. I looked down and...." I turn his hand over and trace the lines of veins on the back of it. "I memorized every hair, every line, every callous. I left for college, and my first ever sex dream was about those hands."

"Whoa, Cara."

I flip his hand palm up once more and lower my lips, kissing the tip of his index finger.

My eyes rise to meet his while I do this, and I see the rapid rise and fall of his chest. "Sweetheart. You didn't... you didn't...wait for me. Tell me you didn't. Not through four years of college and...."

I shake my head and move on to the tip of his middle finger, this time gently kissing and sucking it to the first knuckle.

"Thank god," he breathes.

"I didn't wait," I say when I let go of his finger. "You were in my dreams every night. So it never felt like waiting. These fingers, these hands, that built skyscrapers," I say, kissing his ring finger down to the second knuckle, "were claiming my body every night in my wet dreams."

Michael curses, yanks his hands away from my grip, and runs his fingers along his scalp. His hair gets even more mussed in the process, making him look ten times sexier.

And the next thing I know, with those hands, those lips, he changes my whole world.

# Chapter Five

Michael

I CAN'T TAKE it anymore. I need to feel those soft lips against mine and that soft body pressed against me.

Dammit, why does she have to be so soft and beautiful, and so young?

My mouth claims her with a gentle kiss, because if I take more than that, I won't be able to stop myself from wrecking this precious girl's entire life.

A simple kiss is all she wants from her childhood crush. A simple kiss, I can handle.

Cara's lips against mine are softer and sweeter than I ever could have imagined.

I pull away from the kiss to check on her. "Okay?"

Chuckling, she replies, "I'm so happy you kissed me I might fly away."

"Don't fly away, sweetheart. I need you here with me."

Our mouths meet in the middle. Surely anyone walking their dog can see us kissing if they look closely at my recessed entryway. But at the moment, I don't know if I care. She sighs into my mouth, and it's so sweet I might not be able to hold back the full force of my need much longer. I have to have her. I pull her tight against me, the soft diaphanous sundress sparking a strange new arousal against my bare skin.

She kisses back with lips that taste like cherries, tempting me to open her up and taste more, take everything. Take what doesn't belong to me.

All of the reasons not to kiss her and touch her make me want all of her even more.

The way she moans softly into my mouth when I haven't even slipped her my tongue yet is so pure and sexy I can't stand it.

The sun is shining behind her, casting a silhouette through her sundress that's hardening my dick like steel rebar. I'm utterly in agony, looking at the space between her thighs, wondering, imagining.

"Sweetheart," I say, kissing her cheeks and her forehead, delivering a warning to her even as I can feel her nipples harden against me with our contact. "I don't think you have the slightest idea what a man like me could do to you."

"You've no idea how ready I am for it."

I wet my lips. I'm so hungry to kiss her again. But I need her to know what she's getting herself into. "Oh, are you now?" I growl, roughly hiking up the front of the sundress and flattening my palm against her stomach.

Her tiny gasp at the sudden contact, the widening of her eyes, adds another inch of length to my already aching cock. Not to mention the slight pooch of her soft tummy—the spot I can envision filled with my baby. I would never stop fondling Cara's tummy if—ah fuck I'm setting myself up for more trouble by the second.

I could drag her inside and shut out the world. Keep the prying eyes of Fox Chase away. But once that door closes behind us, she's not leaving again. I leave it open for now. To give her options, and to be a little bit naughty in public, if I'm honest.

"Has anyone ever touched you like this before, sweetheart?" I say, smoothing my fingers down to the waistband of her panties.

Cara's flushed lips part; her nostrils flare. "Only you. You in my dreams, Mr....Michael."

My hand travels lower, discovering the front of her pussy bare.

"Next question. Why don't you have any hair down here?"

Her eyes flutter closed as my hand massages her sensitive skin.

"It's embarrassing, but…I sweat a lot, and it's just more comfortable for me this way."

My other hand props me up against the doorframe, though that hand itches to reach around, cup her jiggly bits and drag her inside. I just want to be bad a bit longer.

"Good answer. Don't ever remove hair just because a man likes you bare. Real men know the sexiest thing in the world is when a woman feels comfortable."

Eyes still closed, she hums a barely audible, "Mmkay."

The contact of my middle finger to the top of her split nearly does me in. The heat, the dampness, the flush of pink spreading across her chest.

"Any man ever touch you here?"

Shaking her head no, Cara bites back a moan, egging me on farther, deeper, my greedy hand exploring her folds.

Her silky wetness is beautiful, demanding more from me. Demanding I keep going. A whimper, and an involuntary jerk of her body, give me pause. If I keep going like this, she's going to come right here on my front porch.

Carefully avoiding her clit, I take my chances and sink the tip of one finger into the source of her heat.

"How about like this?" I ask, plunging deeper, stretching her. She sucks in a breath, and I feel her pussy clamp down around my finger.

"No, no, never. I told you I've been saving it for you, and I meant all of it."

I have to bite my tongue to keep from saying things I shouldn't say. Sweet things. Caveman things. Love things. This isn't about any of that; this is just two adults being filthy.

It tortures me more than it tortures her when I pull out and lean away. Her eyes fly open.

# Chapter Six

Cara

Out of breath and barely capable of speaking, I stare at my torturer. Have I done something wrong?

I open my mouth to speak, but he already has answers before I can voice my questions.

"You won't like it. You won't like the way I need it."

My breath catches in my throat. "I want it all the ways you need it. As long as it's me."

"It won't be nice. It won't be what you deserve. You deserve a prince who will sweep you off your feet and whisper sweet nothings. My brain is full of nothing but filth when I think about you, Cara. And that's wrong. Because you're a sweetheart."

I gird up my loins and say the only thing that will get through to him. "Fuck all of that. Fuck sweet innocent Cara."

Crowding in as close as I can, I block the view of him from the waist down from the street and grab his hand, the one that was just about to make me come. I use it to cover one of my breasts. He needs to feel how hard my nipples are. He needs to know how I crave his touch everywhere.

"Sweet Jesus," he rumbles.

"You've been staring at my breasts all morning. Have at it, then. Have your way with me. Take me on the front lawn for all I care. Let Mrs. Hurley watch. I'm so fucking horny I don't give a shit about anything anymore."

Michael's skin looks taut around his skull, like a beast ready to explode. "So you're saying, I can get you out of my system, and you get me out of my system, and we go back to being functional adults?"

"Yes," I lie.

No way I'm going backward after this. I already predict everything that happens today will only make me love him more.

Brazenly, I reach out and palm his dick. Michael growls from somewhere deep in his chest, barely audible. It's more of a vibration. His eyes take on a wild look as his dick twitches in my hand.

At this exact moment, the sprinklers go off next door at the Hurleys' house. I startle at the noise and then laugh when I realize what it is.

Seeing my laughter, combined with my hand on his length, Michael curses loudly—so loud it echoes off the other houses—then grabs me by both shoulders and pulls me inside.

*Finally*, my heart cries. *Finally.*

His large body slams me against the closed door, his breath all over my neck. "This is it; there's no going back out there, little girl. I'm taking everything."

His hot mouth crashes into mine, and it feels like a million stars explode in my sky. He kisses me hard, fiercely, like a man starved of love and affection.

His hands take control of my body, one pinning both my wrists against the door above my head, the other roughly scraping up the outside of my thigh, hitching up my dress. Michael owns every inch of me he touches.

He deepens the kiss, teasing my mouth open with his tongue. I hadn't had enough of the initial, sweet kissing, but my body is so in tune with him that it responds to the probing of his long, greedy tongue.

With his wet, warm kisses owning my mouth, his hand travels across the front of my thigh and between, urging me to spread my legs. When I do, his palm crosses over the front of my pussy, his calloused hand roughly snagging on the stretchy fabric of my lacy undies.

He groans into my mouth and breaks the kiss, both of us out of breath. His gaze is so intense as his hand brushes back and forth there, below my navel, lighting up every spark of pleasure in my body. I don't know where to look, so I cast my eyes over his shoulder, focusing on the cake on the kitchen table. "Eyes on me, beauty," he rasps.

He demands that we maintain eye contact throughout the next few moments of him gauging my arousal, prodding it, exploring it. It's uncomfortable and yet hot as hell.

His fingers tug the fabric to the side, and he slips two thick digits into my folds. "Is that for me? Is that virgin pussy wet for me? This is what you came here for, isn't it? If you can't look at me while I bang you, then you're not ready, baby girl."

I jut my chin out, rocking my hips forward to increase the pressure of his touch. "I'm ready to be your grown-ass woman."

He arches an eyebrow at me and drags a second, then a third finger through my wetness.

"A grown-ass woman who knows what her man needs.

A grown-ass woman who listens? Who's going to do exactly as I say?"

My lips ache with the need to kiss him again; my pussy throbs as it chases the touch of his exploring hands. "You know I'll do anything."

I let go of her wrists. "Take off that dress."

"Easy," I sigh with a smirk, and the yellow nothing of a dress hits the wall and floats to the hardwood floor.

# Chapter Seven

Michael

My big hand captures her wrists once more above her small frame. I kiss that saucy look right off her sweet face, grinding my body against all of that nearly bare flesh.

Her arms tense up under my hold; her body wriggles. "Be still, Cara."

She whines, "I want to touch you."

I whisper in her ear as my middle finger that's still inside her teases and stretches in circles. "Not yet."

From her ear, I blaze a trail of sloppy kisses down her neck, then soak the thin material of her bra as I take my sweet time to tease each breast on my way down.

"If I let go of your wrists, and you keep your hands to yourself, I'll give you a very special dessert, sweetheart."

She hums her consent. "Mmhmm. I'll try."

I kneel in front of this tiny goddess and take hold of the flimsy red string of her panties between my teeth, and I rip them to smithereens. I shove the lacy souvenir into the pocket of my pajama bottoms, then deliver more sloppy kisses up one leg and down the other.

I have only one more word left in my vocabulary. "Spread."

With her arms clutched together behind her back, Cara widens her stance for me. She's such a good girl. I kiss across the front of her pussy, and she bucks into me.

I look up and notice her eyes are closed; I refuse to make another move until she makes eye contact. Moaning, she wets her lips with her slick pink tongue. Her pussy presses against my face, begging for mercy.

"Eyes on me, baby girl."

Her eyes fly open, and my sweet, innocent Cara is transformed. She's a wanton hussy in this moment, and I could not love it more. With our eyes locked together, I strum her clit with my tongue. My little Cara's eyes glaze over, and her lips flood with heat. I stroke her taut button two, three more times, and her body seizes. Her cunt clamps down around my fingers, and I tease her through her first orgasm with me.

I don't stop touching or petting her. I don't ever want to.

When I come back to standing, I push my two wet fingers into her mouth, watching the way Cara's mouth grabs onto them, sucking and licking, a questioning look in her eye. She needs me to tell her she's doing it right. "Good girl. Now share it with me."

She moans against my mouth as I delve my tongue into hers. Her tight body still shivers through the aftershocks.

I fall to my knees once again and spread her thighs open some more, tossing one of her legs over my shoulder, then the other.

"Now. Now you hold on to me, sweetness."

Cara lets out a small squeak of surprise when I pierce

through her folds with my tongue, claiming what's mine, then sighs. "Oh my god, Michael. Ohmygod, ohmygod, ohmygod."

She's bucking against my face again, and I laugh wickedly, knowing that naughty little clit likes what I did to it the first time, and it wants more. Her hands get lost in my hair; the more I delve and explore her with my mouth, the more she tugs. I recall the memory from just this morning before I realized who she was. I'd wanted to die between these thighs, and I maintain this position. She could snap my neck, and I'd die happy.

My good girl's thighs begin to shake, and I know she's ready. I help her carefully slide her legs down as I come to standing.

"Now, you're ready," I whisper into her neck, encouraging her to grab onto my shoulders. I hike her soft thighs up high around my waist and rub the tip of my cock through her folds, coating myself in her juice.

"I'm gonna fuck you so good, baby girl."

She arcs against me, and I slip the tip in, getting her used to me. Once she adjusts, and I'm ready to sink in deeper, another rude visitor from the outside world begins to bang on my door.

I'm about to tell Mrs. Hurley to jump in a lake, but the voice that accompanies the knocking is not Mrs. Hurley.

"Cara? Are you going to help me clean up?"

Cara's eyes fly open in fright, and she mouths silently. "Diana!"

I smile and kiss her deeply sensuously, then murmur in her ear, "I told you once you come inside, you can't leave."

"She might need my help," she whispers.

"Fuck that," I say. "Let her clean it up herself."

Cara's eyes flash at me, and she bites her lip wickedly.

Then she calls through the door to her sister. "The bins are in the gar—ohmygod! Garage."

Me being the filthy old man that I am, I press in an inch deeper while she explains through the door where to stow decorations.

Diana is annoyed. If only she knew what we're up to on the other side of this door.

"Excuse me? Are you coming out to help me or not?"

I break through her final barrier, and Cara bites her lip and cries out in a small, barely audible whimper. Her eyes squeeze shut, and I see a tear form in the corner of her eye. I kiss it away. "N-not!" she manages to shout.

"Excellent," I growl quietly as I pull out and slide back in, all the way to the hilt. Her thighs squeeze my waist, her feet are clenched together at the ankles at the small of my back, commanding me to drive in deeper.

I hear Diana scoff and say, "Fine. Screw you then." Her footsteps disappear, and I lunge forward, thrusting hard into my girl.

"Happily," I say. "Think I'll do just that."

I can't remember the last time I had skin-on-skin sex without a condom, and it's fucking delicious.

"So tight I can barely take it. So tight, so fucking tight."

For Cara's part, her body crashes against me, looking for friction. Her needy clit needs more from me.

I reach down between us and let her clit have it while I bang her against the door, again and again. With every thrust, she lets go a little more. Opens up for me a little more. Grips me a little tighter.

Everything about what I'm feeling is too much. I know it's wrong, and the wrongness makes me want Cara more.

Her ass is as soft under that sundress as I imagined and even more so. She's so soft and willing and sweet as lemon meringue; I fear I might fuck her through the door. But her body and her gaze tell me differently.

The rolling of her hips matches the frenzy of my thrusts. She's getting the hang of this shockingly fast. I palm her ass with one hand and anchor us both with the other arm against the door as I drive in, again and again, building a sensual rhythm.

I mouth her breasts, one then the other, throughout my fervent thrusts.

The release nearly knocks me off my feet, but she takes all of it, her pussy clamping down and taking in every inch of my cock and every drop of my cum.

The broken part of my brain wishes she wasn't on birth control. The dark monster inside me wishes she was in my cave, she was my virgin bride, and we were here together, with nothing else to do but make babies.

My shoulders shudder with the last spurt into her welcoming heat.

I'm a monster for waiting until I took her virginity to tell her the truth about me. But I have to say it. She looks up at me with a fresh flush of red blazing across her face, a glint in her eye, and wantonly mussed hair.

Here goes nothing.

# Chapter Eight

Cara

"That's it?"

I look up at him as we sit on the end of Michael's bed, with me curled up in his lap. He was so sweet with me afterward, helping me put my dress back on and smoothing out my hair, and not even laughing at me when I didn't know what to say after sex.

"Thank you," I'd said. He'd only smiled and kissed me on the neck. That was the third or fourth time he'd done that since he pulled me into his house. But he was not precisely kissing my neck. Kissing and inhaling and making strange, caveman noises, like he wanted to burrow inside me via my collarbone. Like I possess something in that spot that promises to blot out the world.

And now, sitting in his lap, I'm listening to him tell me what he needs from me, now that I've allowed him to draw me into his world. "That's it? That's all you need me to do?"

"Uh. Yeah, that's it," he says, lifting one shoulder.

I can't believe what I'm hearing. I blow out a breath of relief. "I thought it was going to be hardcore. I don't care what anybody is into, but as a sexual novice, I'm relieved," I say.

Michael blinks at me like I've just given him the crown jewels. "You would be surprised at how many women have never talked to me again after learning about my kink."

I run a hand over his face and neck and down his chest. "I don't think it's that weird to ask for husband/wife role play."

"It's a little too weird for a lot of people."

Inside, I'm jumping up and down. Playing house with this man? I've been doing that in my head since I was twelve. Not a problem for me at all.

"It feels like the thing that you've always wanted manifesting in this kink, and now it's hardwired."

"You're a wise old soul," he says.

I slide off his lap and say, "Nah. I minored in psych. Let's eat some cake."

Cara

"YOU DON'T HAVE to do all this," Michael says when I hand him a plate that I whipped up from the meager contents of his fridge. A low-fat cheese and egg white omelet, fruit, and of course, a slice of cake.

I laugh. "You said you wanted to role play. Let's do it."

He acquiesces and digs in, emitting adorable yum-yum noises over my cooking. Not going to lie; this roleplay is convincing on his part.

"And besides, you need to eat something healthy before you go into a diabetic coma. You can't have cake for breakfast at your age, Mr. Brennan."

He laughs ruefully at the reminder.

"I'm sorry," I say. "I didn't mean…."

"It's fine. You're right. I asked for wife role play, and this is pretty method," he says with a smile and a wink.

I drink my glass of juice. "A wife needs to take care of her man."

"I agree."

"It's easy with you. I always liked your eyes. I thought they were kind. And you're funny, the way you bust my dad's chops."

"We could maybe not talk about your dad," he says.

"Of course. I'm sorry."

I must look more remorseful than intended because Michael reaches across the table and pulls me into his lap for a kiss.

"I should not have asked you to refrain from talking about your family. Sooner or later, this subject is going to come up."

My heart races for a brief moment, wondering if he means this for real, as in, we'll have to figure out how to tell my parents about our relationship.

"I mean, talking about our age differences and the whole aspect of me being your dad's best friend can only make the roleplay hotter, right?"

I swallow, my hopes dashed, and nod bravely. "Absolutely."

"Hey," he says, touching my chin. "Just tell me if this is too much for you."

I should tell him that, of course, it's too much for me. Because the truth is, I love him. I love this man with all my heart. He can pretend to be a monster, but I just saw what he did for the preschool kids and me. My heart is full of love for him, and if this is a temporary thing, the heartbreak will crush me.

"I want to be whatever you need me to be," I say. "So, my sweet husband, tell me. What would you have been doing this beautiful Saturday morning if Mrs. Hurley hadn't come knocking on your door?"

He gives a slight shrug and says, "Honestly, I don't know. It's not as if the days of the week matter anymore when you don't go into the office on Monday through Friday. Come to think of it, Saturdays didn't mean all that much when I worked sixty-hour weeks, either. Not since childhood has Saturday been anything but a concept."

I know this wealthy, powerful, and sexy man does not want my pity. But I can't help but feel bad at how he's spent his whole life working so hard with no warm home life to look forward to on weekends.

"I'm sorry I interrupted your Saturday, regardless, with my tacky cakewalk. I didn't know it wasn't allowed."

Michael scoffs. "You know what bothers me even more? Snobs. If I didn't think Mrs. Hurley would cause trouble for your family, I would have let it slide. Sweetheart, whatever you need from now on, you come to me. I want your weekends free from now on."

Is this the honest Michael or play-husband Michael? I try to hide the shaking of my breath. "Surely you have exciting guy things to do on weekends, now that you're retired."

"Cara, I don't camp or hunt or fish or whatever it is that dudes do on their days off. Of course, that didn't stop me from wanting to build a cabin in the woods."

I lean back in surprise. "A cabin? I didn't know you wanted a cabin."

"Of course you did. You're my wife; you know everything."

I chuckle at how cute he's being.

"And if I were there right now, I would still be sleeping."

"Or making love to your wife. Unless this is a hunting cabin, then I can't go there."

He shakes his head. "No, just a cabin to get away from people."

I laugh. "That sounds more like the Michael I know.

Michael on the outside. Michael on the inside is a lovely, squishy fellow. Otherwise, Corinna and Bill would never have been friends with you."

"They are the best people," he says. "I never would have sold my condo in the city and moved to the 'burbs if it weren't for them. I wasn't all that sure about it at first, but I somehow convinced myself that the clubhouse membership and the space were worth it. Build a big house, and a wife will come along, and soon after that, kids."

I swallow. "Here I am!" I chirp, only half-joking. *Oh god, what am I doing to myself?*

"So tell me. How does my wife spend her time when not letting this old man sully her virtue?"

I heave a long sigh and look up at the plaster medallion in the ceiling. "With my pre-K kids, and figuring out how to make the most of the meager resources. With the PTA focused solely on the needs of traditional K-8, the principal, Mrs. Walker, needs volunteers to be in charge of organizing all pre-K fundraising for the time being. And with me being the most junior member of the faculty at the age of 23, how could I say no? Besides, I adore all the kids at this school, and I would do anything to help them."

He listens and then clears his throat. "Those kids' teachers aren't going to need to worry about money ever again."

I cock my head. "That's very sweet of you, husband, but you can't singlehandedly fund an entire wing of the school."

"Watch me."

I don't know how to react to this. "This is a very different Michael than the one who shows himself to the world."

"And you're very different from the girl who used to

squeak and run away like a bunny whenever I would talk to her.

If we're going to do this thing, I can't have you shying away, Cara. Can you handle coming to me at any time, anywhere, when I need you? No questions asked?"

I chuckle, "Well, I do have a job."

"You don't need it."

I rear back. Is this real, or is this the role play? "Sir. I didn't go to four years of college just to not teach. I love those kids."

"Fine," he sighs. "But when you come home to me, I want you wearing skirts and dresses so I can fuck you whenever I need you, as soon as you walk in the door."

My body shivers in response to the memory of what we just did. He wrecked me so hard I can still almost feel him inside me. "Yes, Mr. Brennan."

"And I want you in my bed at night because that's where wives belong. Where I can reach for you and fuck you slowly in the middle of the night."

His dirty words knock the wind out of me. I take hold of his face and kiss him with everything I'm feeling. Hoping he'll understand how I feel, hoping the connection will give me back my words, my breath, and my senses.

I pull away from the kiss and begin to trace kisses down his neck and across his chest. I slide off his lap and get on the floor in front of him.

But before my knees hit the floor, Michael catches me.

"No. Stand up, Cara."

"But I want to make my husband feel good after being so good to me this morning."

Michael sweeps me entirely off my feet, and before I understand what's happening, we're marching to the bedroom, him carrying me in his arms like it's our honeymoon. If only.

His voice is ragged again. "You want that? You better believe you're not going to be on your knees when you get it."

His roughness, assertiveness catches me off guard but also sends my sex twitching with the need for him all over again. "But I thought that's how...."

He tosses me on the bed, crawls over me, and crashes his mouth against mine.

I let out a quiet yip of surprise. "Did I hurt you?" he asks.

I pull him back to me and answer, "Nuh-uh," without breaking the kiss.

"Here," he says. "Here is where my wife gives me my post-breakfast blowjob."

He stands to rid himself of his pajama bottoms—finally. I can't wait to wash them along with all of the laundry I can find. For the roleplay, of course.

This whole scenario is fucking with me in so many different ways, and I don't understand why I want to do this man's dirty laundry. My sisters would be shocked. Diana and Cecily, the most feminist of our family, especially would bite my head off.

"Be patient with me," I say, watching this long, thick man spread-eagle on the bed, completely naked, his thick, pink member rising to attention in slow, languorous pulses. He pats the bed next to him. "Lie down however you're comfortable, and I'll talk you through it."

With one hand caressing my bare bottom under my sundress, Michael is so kind and tender with me while I suck him off.

I always had a feeling I would end up in tears if I ever gave someone a blowjob. I just never imagined it would be tears full of every emotion one can name.

# Chapter Ten

Michael

I LET it go too far.

Don't get me wrong; playing house with Cara is better than I could have imagined as far as my fantasy fulfillment goes.

Best of all, neither of us answers to anyone, living for the next day and a half in complete pretend domestic bliss.

I don't ask Cara to do anything, but she cooks my meals, washes and folds my laundry, cleans the entire house, and massages my feet while we watch Netflix and chill. To the casual observer, it would seem I have this woman under my thumb. In reality, she takes all the initiative. The more I protest, the more she insists.

She says she loves the role play as much as I do. As evidenced by her unquenchable fire in the bedroom, I believe her.

We fuck in every room of the house, like newlyweds. Or as I imagine, newlyweds should.

We feed each other lemon blueberry cake in the kitchen with every meal, but only after I eat all my vegetables.

I have to mark on a calendar how much water I drink because she wants to make sure I'm hydrated. I'm sloshing around so much that I don't even have room for whiskey on Saturday and Sunday night. And I don't want it, anyway. I want every single second with this woman burned into my brain, clear as the blue of her eyes.

Sunday night comes too soon.

In the shower before bed, her face looks sad, and this is the point at which I think I've taken it too far.

"Talk to me, sweetheart. You look like something is on your mind."

Cara smiles up at me wanly while soaping up a sponge and running it over my chest.

"I don't want to go to work tomorrow," she says.

"So don't go. Simple," I say.

"I mean, I do. I love my job. I just don't want the fantasy to end. There's a lot we haven't discussed—as husband and wife—that we should discuss."

Something in her eyes tells me there's more to this than role play. I've let it go too far, and she's going to get hurt. Let me be perfectly honest—I'm not going to hurt her. This whole thing that I'm into purely for sex has turned into something else. I don't want her to leave. Ever.

"You can say anything to me, lovely."

"I know this is a game to you, but I have news. I didn't take my birth control pill today."

At this moment, I make the wrong choice. I think I'm doing the right thing by listening, but instead, she takes it as shocked silence. Inside, I'm cautiously pleased. I want nothing else but to have this woman, pregnant, in my bed —every night.

I take the sponge from her and lather it up, rubbing it over her back, massaging her shoulders while we share a silence.

I should have anticipated this, and I should have already decided what to say.

"I…I'm fine with that, Cara."

Her face changes and I know instantly she's putting a mask back on. She lolls her head back and laughs, then points at me. "Gotcha!"

This is what she needs right now, to save face. She nearly let her emotions get the better of her, and she needs to make a joke.

I wish she would just tell me.

That night, I spoon up behind her in bed and wrap her tight in my arms.

She sighs. I lose myself in her hair.

"What's my retired husband going to do tomorrow?"

"Oh, probably go 18 holes with Bill. Or probably get my teeth knocked out by his five iron."

"Maybe don't tell him you married his daughter and instead have a nice 18 holes, my love."

The way she says "my love" grips me, squeezes all the juice out of my heart.

I want to hear her say it again. Every day. For the rest of my life.

# Chapter Eleven

Cara

WHEN I ARRIVE at school the following day, I hand the checks over to the school principal on my way to my classroom.

"You sold some cake!" Mrs. Walker says, examining the checks.

"I sold some of them twice," I say, adding, "never mind," when she throws me a curious look.

"Why are these checks both from a Michael Brennan?"

I explain to her how it all played out, and she looks bewildered but waves me off. "Whatever gets the job done. Thank you."

I head to my sensory play classroom early and fire up my laptop as I sit at a kid-sized table surrounded by bean-bag chairs, soothing lights, and play tunnels. I don't mind not having a desk or an office; this classroom is my happy place. *Well, now it's maybe your second-happiest place,* I think, setting aside the fact that I might be the only person in my relationship with Michael letting the husband/wife play get into her head. Then the horrifying thought occurs to me: *what if there's more than one? The man is experienced, has a strong sex drive, and all the time in the world on his hands. What if I've just let myself become one of several women at his beck and call? What if…*

As I recall, he'd said, "You'd be surprised at how many women hate it." But that doesn't necessarily mean…

*Stop it. Stop it, and get on with your day. Later, you can grow a spine and come right out and ask. And then, you can deal with the fallout later. If he breaks your heart, consider yourself lucky that you have four sisters to run to with your problems.*

Taking several deep breaths, I get on with my work. The leading teaching team and the other assistants will be here soon, and I want to tackle my weekend email beforehand. When I finish with that, I log in to the shared spreadsheet on all the upcoming pre-K fundraisers for the school year.

"That's odd," I mutter out loud to myself.

Every date is blank. The cookie dough sale, the wrapping paper sale, the silent auction, even the book fair. Thinking I must have logged into the wrong file, I check again. But no, this is the one.

I shoot an email to the lead teacher, apologizing that something must have corrupted the file but that I'll put it back together today.

Just as I hit "send," there's a knock on the open classroom door. I look up, and there's an enormous delivery of yellow daisies—so massive I can't even see the face of the delivery person. "Cara Williams?"

"Yes?"

She comes in and sets the glass vase of flowers on the tiny table in front of me and has me sign for the delivery. "I'm sorry, I don't have anything on me to tip you with."

The delivery driver waves me off. "Don't worry about it, honey. That man of yours already tipped me enough to cancel my credit card debt. I don't know what the flowers are for, but I suggest you hang on to this one." She practically skips out of the room, and I snatch the card buried inside the bouquet.

"These reminded me of you," is all it says.

I blush and smile, remembering how many ways Michael violated my yellow daisy sundress.

Then something the delivery driver said gets my attention. He canceled her credit card debt? Based on his actions on Saturday, I believe it. But does that mean…

I look back at the blank fundraiser spreadsheet, and at that moment, I receive a call from the lead teacher, who is on her way in. "Got your email. All the fundraisers have been canceled as of this morning. An anonymous benefactor has set up a trust fund for the entire Exceptional Pre-K department. I'm running late because Walker just got emergency approval from the super to post three new teacher positions for us, and she wanted my input."

I have to pick my jaw up off the floor when we end the phone call, and I immediately call up Michael.

"Good morning, baby girl." He sounds like he's still in bed, and my aching muscles would like to crawl back under the sheets with him right now.

"You've been busy," I say.

He laughs. "Nah. My accountants have been busy. Now you're exceedingly not busy, and you never have to head up another fundraiser again. Nobody in your department will. And apart from teaching, I get you all to myself."

In the background, I hear knocking on his door.

*It could be another one of his pets.*

I bite my lip. "You gotta go?"

"Yeah, more HOA bullshit, probably. But Cara?"

"Yes?"

"I…I miss you."

It feels like he means it. It doesn't sound like someone with a corral full of women. There was real emotion there. Almost like he wanted to say more.

"I miss you too."

"Come see me as soon as you're off work."

Every muscle below my waist tightens at the promise behind that command. I bite down on my lip to control the whimper of need. My heart knows we need to have a serious talk. The rest of me wants another night of mind-blowing orgasms before approaching that subject.

---

"I want you to stop taking the pill."

I blink up at Michael in astonishment. I've done exactly as he said: appeared at his door just minutes after getting off work, with a stop on the way here for groceries, both because he needs them and because I'm getting into the wife character. *And because you love him, silly girl.*

"That's a fun game. Adding Russian roulette to the role play, are we?"

I smile and brush past him and head to the kitchen to stock his pantry.

"Cara. I don't want to roleplay anymore."

I whirl around, hurt but also confused. "You want me to go because I questioned your birth control suggestion?"

Now Michael looks confused. "What? No. I meant what I said."

There's a slight lump in my throat that's beginning to bubble up. "Okay, sweetheart. I'll 'stop taking birth control' for you, my husband."

Both of us are thoroughly confused now.

"We're not doing this anymore," he says.

*Do not cry in front of this man, Cara.* Bravely, I nod and say, "I'm sure one of your other female friends does a better job at pretending and not falling in love with the idea of the real thing."

Michael scrapes his fingers through his hair, then grabs me under my arm and marches me through the house and into the backyard. Outside, by the pool, he takes a knee and pulls out a tiny red box.

"This is some elaborate roleplay."

"Cara, I did this all wrong. I don't want to do the role play anymore because I want you for real. There's nobody else in my life. Nobody has ever broken through to my real heart. You're it for me. I want you as my wife. And I want babies with you. As soon as possible."

That lump in my throat grows bigger by the second.

"I need you to back up a minute because I need to catch my breath."

"Marry me. I love you, Cara, and I want you to marry me. This isn't your pretend husband asking. This is me, Michael, your dad's best friend, asking you to marry me."

He opens the small red box, but I'm suddenly feeling faint because I'm hyperventilating.

"Is this real or the matrix? I can't decide," I breathe.

Sensing my weakened state, Michael stands and catches me quickly, wrapping me up in his strong arms, caging me in from the world.

"Dammit, woman. I should never have suggested role play. I should have just asked you to marry me the second I realized it was you in that daisy-yellow dress because I knew I would never think of anyone else in the same way as you. You're in my head and in my heart, little one."

I let him kiss me, and I kiss him back.

"You know what we have to do now," I say.

He nods solemnly. "Right. You stay here. I'll speak to your parents. They arrived back from vacation this morning."

I shake my head. "No, sir. This is all part of being a grown-ass woman. Facing the music with my real-life husband."

# Chapter Twelve

Michael

"Well, Mom and Dad," Diana says, arms crossed, an amused look on her face, "At least they didn't ruin your vacation."

Cara glowers at her sister, but it's Chloe—attending the Williams family meeting via FaceTime from Warwickshire—who reins in the middle child. "Diana. Let's just hear what they have to say. After all, Cara's not the first person to fall for an older gentleman."

"Don't remind me," Cecily says, shuddering in her armchair in the Williams' three-season porch. Apparently, this serene deck with its pretty wicker furniture surrounded by soothing greenery and bird feeders is where the Williams all prefer to go when they need to hash out complex subjects. Or extremely awkward ones, such as best friends proposing marriage to daughters half their age.

Cecily being the youngest and the most outspoken, I'm

not surprised by her reaction. Diana has been aware of Cara's crush for years. Cherise is oddly quiet and sits on her hands, making eye contact with no one, instead focusing on some hummingbirds buzzing around.

As for the opinions that count the most—that of Corrina and Bill—I just have to wait.

After Cara had requested the family meeting, I thought it best to be as straightforward as possible.

"I love your daughter, and we're going to be married. As soon as possible," I'd said at the outset.

Bill and Corrina have been sitting there together on the floral-cushioned wicker love seat in stunned silence for the better part of five minutes while their five girls talk at each other.

"Cecily," Chloe warns, pausing to let Cara point the camera in Cecily's direction. "I thought you'd come around on the idea that age is just a number."

The baby of the family goggles at her oldest, married, and pregnant sister. "No, you all decided we were all fine with this, and I was told I would warm up to the situation. Well, I haven't."

"Cecily, you're going to be an auntie in less than a month."

Cecily throws up her hands and shouts, "I'm twenty-one! I'm too young to be an aunt!"

Cara cuts in. "Why? Mom and Dad had Chloe when they were 19 and 20."

Cecily wretches. "I'm not super cool with that idea, either."

"Maybe not," Cara says, "But you do recognize the fact that they are much younger than most of our friends' parents. Twenty years' difference is not that significant."

Diana scoffs, "Maybe Cecily is just horrified because it seems like gold-digging is starting to run in the family."

"Hey!" Chloe shouts over the phone.

"Stop it, that's not helpful," Corrina says over Chloe's shouts. And in the next moment, the entire meeting has devolved into shouting and name-calling and arguing.

Bill still looks stunned and silent. Finally, I catch his eye, but his expression is unreadable.

Finally, it's Cara—sweet, soft-spoken, innocent Cara—who commands everyone to be quiet. "Everyone shut up!"

Surprised, everyone quiets down and gives Cara the floor.

"I know this is uncomfortable considering Michael's friendship with Dad. And Dad, I know this is a shock, and you might even feel betrayed. But I want you to promise me you won't take it out on Michael. I…well, Diana already knows this, but I've had a crush on Michael forever. He never once—never—looked or said or did anything inappropriate with me. Not ever. We hadn't seen each other in four years, and then we ran into each other on Saturday. And to be honest, I instigated things."

"What do you mean, instigated?" Corrina questions.

Cara juts out one sassy hip and says, "Mother, I seduced him. So if you're angry with anyone, be angry with me."

Corinna blows out a breath and slumps back into the seat cushions, processing.

"Bill," I say. "I'm going to need you to say something. Anything."

Bill stands and says, "I need a drink for this," and leaves the room.

I follow him and leave the Williams women to hash things out among themselves.

When I arrive in the kitchen, Bill is halfway through a can of beer, and I don't begrudge him not offering one to me.

Having grabbed a second can for himself, he slams the fridge door and glares at me.

"You want to hit me? I'd prefer you hit me instead of silence."

Bill swallows his gulp of beer and says, "I heard you're subsidizing the entire special education department."

I clarify, "The pre-K section, but yeah. Sort of."

"Why? To impress my daughter? To give my daughter permission to go after her dad's best friend?"

I shake my head no. "Because whatever she loves, I love. Because whatever Cara's passionate about, I'm passionate about."

"No disrespect, but you've never been passionate about anything except building skyscrapers and making money."

"Is that what you think of me?"

"No," Bill says, taking another sip of beer. "But we're all going to need a minute. Can you give us that?"

"Anything you need, I'm there. Cara cares about your opinion more than anyone else's, and I want to make sure, even if we're not friends anymore, that you can continue to have a relationship with your daughter."

Bill taps the bottle against his bottom lip, then says, "You do realize how this is very different from Chloe and Phillip? Even though he's even older than you?"

"I do," I say, hoping against hope that I'll get to hold on to the essential people in my world: Cara and her parents.

Finally, Bill crosses to me and holds out his hand to shake mine. I heave a sigh of relief. "This isn't my blessing. This is just me letting you know I'll be okay, eventually. A pre-blessing."

Dammit, why is my face wet? All I can do is wipe my stupid eyes on my stupid shirt sleeve and thank him.

"WHAT ELSE DID HE SAY?"

My Cara and I stroll down Hunter Drive at dusk, going over the events of the evening. The sun sets over the golf course in the distance, and teenagers are out walking their dogs. Even I have to admit; this can be a nice neighborhood. Sometimes.

"That's it. He just needs time," I say.

Cara presses me, wanting to know the exact wording, facial expressions, body language, and tone. And I tell her everything I can remember.

"You're killing me, Mr. Brennan," she laughs.

"Remind me to get better at observing people if this is how conversations are going to go for the rest of our lives together."

She stops in front of the Hurleys' yard and presses against me, weaving her fingers through mine. "I hope that doesn't make you sad."

I squeeze her fingers. "What are you talking about?"

"The rest of our lives. If I have a baby, you'll be in your sixties when they graduate high school."

I pull her tighter against me, aware this is the first time we've shown public affection, apart from groping each other in my doorway, of course. We're probably going to have to get used to people staring at us.

"Weren't you the one who told me to stop doing the math and just be happy?" I remind her.

"I am happy," she says. "Unless this is an elaborate roleplay in which you've enlisted my family, so if that's the case...."

Her face is too close and too anxious for me not to hush her up with my kiss. Grabbing her tight to me without a care in the world, I claim my bride's mouth with mine. My bride that I'm going to get pregnant tonight if I have anything to say about it.

Bill might need time, but as far as I'm concerned, I can't start living my authentic life soon enough.

As we kiss, we're both suddenly surprised as the Hurleys' lawn sprinklers pop up and start spurting cold water all over us.

Shrieking and laughing, Cara tries to dash off to my house—or our house, as I see it. But I pull her back to me and lift her feet off the sidewalk in another deep, mind-melding kiss. She sighs against me, and when we pull away, we're both soaked to the skin.

My Cara has a wicked look in her eye and tugs me toward the grass.

"What are you doing?" I ask, watching her let go of me to run circles around the sprinklers, jumping and dancing in the water.

"Uh, it's not that kind of sprinkler," I say, noting how I'm going to have to pay for the Hurleys to re-lay that fresh sod she's trampling right now.

"Come on, don't be such a fussy old lady," she calls. Her white dress is completely soaked through, and the peepshow is too much for public consumption. Just then, Mrs. Hurley steps outside to inspect the current commotion.

"Ah, fuck it," I say and join my wife. I hold her in my arms as we twirl through the water, laughing, snorting, and getting completely soaked.

"I love you, Mrs. Brennan," I say.

"I know!" Cara shouts, then turns to Mrs. Hurley. "Did you hear that? Mr. Brennan loves me, and I love him! Isn't it wonderful?"

Mrs. Hurley splutters, then pulls out her phone to call…who, I wonder? Security?

Her door slams as she goes back inside the house, and Cara turns to me. "You know, we might have to move," she says.

"One hundred percent," I say in agreement. "Anywhere, as long as you're with me."

# Epilogue

Cara

Five years later

I'm nervously pacing the floor on Christmas Eve. I'm praying everything is okay with baby number three, but honestly, I'm worried.

Because we all spent last year's Christmas at my brother-in-law's castle, the Williams clan has decided to gather for this year's holiday weekend at Michael's cabin in the woods. Being the one five months pregnant this year, everyone agreed not to put me on an international flight.

"Bit Unabomber out here, isn't it?" asks Diana, who's as snarky as ever, but I've missed getting my chops busted by her on the regular. She's quite tied up lately with her new husband. As for Cherise and Cecily, we're all wondering when their beaus will pop the question. Cherise has been very secretive, and nobody has met her boyfriend yet. Cecily has somewhat followed in Chloe's footsteps with a celebrity chef at her beck and call; the only difference is that A-lister chased her down and sort of stalked her. Yes, she's eating all her words from the time she accused her sisters of gold-digging.

"You should talk," Chloe teases. "You and Antonio holed up in your pizza mansion with more security than a military base."

"Runs in the family," Antonio says, holding out a slice of Phillip's fruitcake to Diana. Suddenly her eyes go wide. "Wow, that's pungent, no thank you."

Antonio snuggles her in close. "None for you, then. I don't want you feeling nauseated on Christmas."

I wonder why Diana's suddenly so snuggly, but I quickly forget as my hand goes to my tummy.

I sip my herbal tea and watch the snow fall gently in the trees.

Suddenly, I feel my husband's warm brick wall of solid support behind me. He slips his arms around me and rests his hands on my tummy. "What's going on in your head today?"

Michael. He always knows when I'm preoccupied.

"I just worry about the little nugget. With Grace and Mikey Junior, I felt them kicking almost like clockwork at five months."

"I'm sure it's fine, but do you want me to call the doctor?"

I shake my head. "No, not tonight."

"When was the last time you ate?"

I have to think about that for a minute. "Um…"

"There's your answer. Here." He hands me a slice of fruitcake, kisses me on the neck, and says he will be right back with some real food.

I sit down in the comfy chair by the window and sip my

tea, then set the suspicious-looking fruitcake aside. I'm pretty sure it's the exact cake from last year that nobody touched.

The brandy aroma alone is enough to make my eyes water. And suddenly, I feel it—the little nugget kicks. I rush from the room to find Michael. "Babe!"

He pops out of the kitchen carrying a tray of dishes. "What? Sweetheart, are you okay?"

I nod vigorously and wave him over. "He's kicking! Baby Will says hello!"

I'm so relieved, and I can tell that Michael is too. "Oh, thank god," he sighs.

Staring at my husband, I say, "I thought you weren't worried?"

Michael kisses my forehead while resting one hand on my tummy, laughing at the little knees, feet, and elbows responding to his voice. "Cara, wife of mine, I worry all day every day whether you're pregnant or not. It's my only job since the day we fell in love."

Diana groans, but everyone eventually sprints over to feel the baby kick. Even Dad.

I look down at all the hands on my tummy, and I'm so happy that this little one is going to join this crazy family soon.

I look up and see Dad and Michael, still friends, having adapted to the new normal.

The truth is, there's nothing normal about our family, and that's just fine with me.

## THE END

*Thank you for reading Cake Walk! If you enjoyed this story, please visit my website at authorabbyknox.com for information on lots more titles to read. Want to know more about Chloe's sister Diana* and her sexy, pizza-chef boss? Read *Hand-Tossed* next. *Homemade Heat* reading order:

*Judge Me*
*Cake Walk*
*Hand-Tossed*
*Chef's Kiss*
*Bite Me*

*Crash into Me (grumpy mountain man)*

*Snowed Under (second chance, later-in-life)*

*Wish List (holiday, older heroine/younger hero)*

*Fate's Holi-Date (he falls first, age gap)*

**Wood Brothers series**

*(OTT alpha insta-love. Set in same world as Roadside Attractions.)*

*Nailed*

*Screwed*

*Drilled*

*Love Games series*

*(OTT insta love, nerdy-but-hot heroes. Set in same world as Roadside Attractions.)*

*Roll For Initiative*

*Roll for Damage*

*Roll for Charisma*

**The Mail-Order Brides of Darling Creek**

*(tropes include: age gap, mail/e-mail order brides, small town, insta love, cowboy)*

*A Baby for the Bride*

*A Week to Wed*

*Her Guardian Groom*

*The Cowboy Auction of Darling Creek*

*(tropes include: dating auction, small town, cowboy, insta love)*

*The Cowgirl's Bid*

*Winning the Cowboy*

*Her Forbidden Prize*

*Small-Town Gossip*

*(Set in Darling Creek, Montana. Tropes include: small town, insta love, workplace romance)*

*Do That To Me*

*Say That To Me*

*Love That For Me*

Paradise Passions

*(vacation romances)*

*Babymoon*

*Honeymoon Hideout*

*Need more stand alones?*

*Are You For Reel?*

*The Bodyguard and His Bunny*

*A Little Amusement*

*511 Kissme Lane*

*V-Card Vacation*

*Hail Mary*

Holiday short reads

*Elf-napped*

*Bagged by the Elf*

*Wish List*

*Snow-plowed*

*The Christmas Pickup*

*The Halloween Bet*

*The Halloween Flip*

*Pumpkin King*

*Snow-plowed*


*Additional titles are available on iBooks, Barnes & Noble, Everand, Smashwords, Fable, and more.*

*For signed paperbacks, exclusive downloads, and more, visit Abby's website at authorabbyknox.com*

*Happy reading!*

www.ingramcontent.com/pod-product-compliance
Lightning Source LLC
Chambersburg PA
CBHW052206150726
48002CB00003B/1136